Rain School

WRITTEN AND ILLUSTRATED BY JAMES RUMFORD

HOUGHTON MIFFLIN BOOKS FOR CHILDREN

Houghton Mifflin Harcourt · Boston · New York · 2010

Dédié à mon ami Doug Hergert
et à sa famille

In the country of Chad, it is the first day of school. The dry dirt road is filling up with children.

Big brothers and big sisters are leading the way.

"Will they give us a notebook?" Thomas asks.
"Will they give us a pencil?"
"Will I learn to read like you?"
"Stop asking so many questions and keep up,"
say the big brothers and big sisters.

Thomas arrives at the schoolyard, but there are no classrooms.
There are no desks.

It doesn't matter.
There is a teacher.
"We will build our school,"
she says. "This is the first lesson."

Thomas learns to make mud bricks and dry them in the sun.

He learns to build mud walls and mud desks.

He gathers grass and saplings with the other children,
and they make a roof.

Inside it is cool. It smells of the earth. It smells of the fields
ready for planting.
Thomas helps bring in little wooden stools.
Everyone sits down.
This is the moment they have been waiting for.

The teacher brings in a blackboard.
On it she writes a letter.
"A!" says the teacher.
"A!" says Thomas with the other children.
The teacher writes the letter with big strokes in the air.
The students do the same, over and over.
"Wonderful," says the teacher.

She hands out notebooks and pencils.
"Page one," says the teacher. Thomas opens
his notebook to the first page and holds his
pencil ready and waiting.

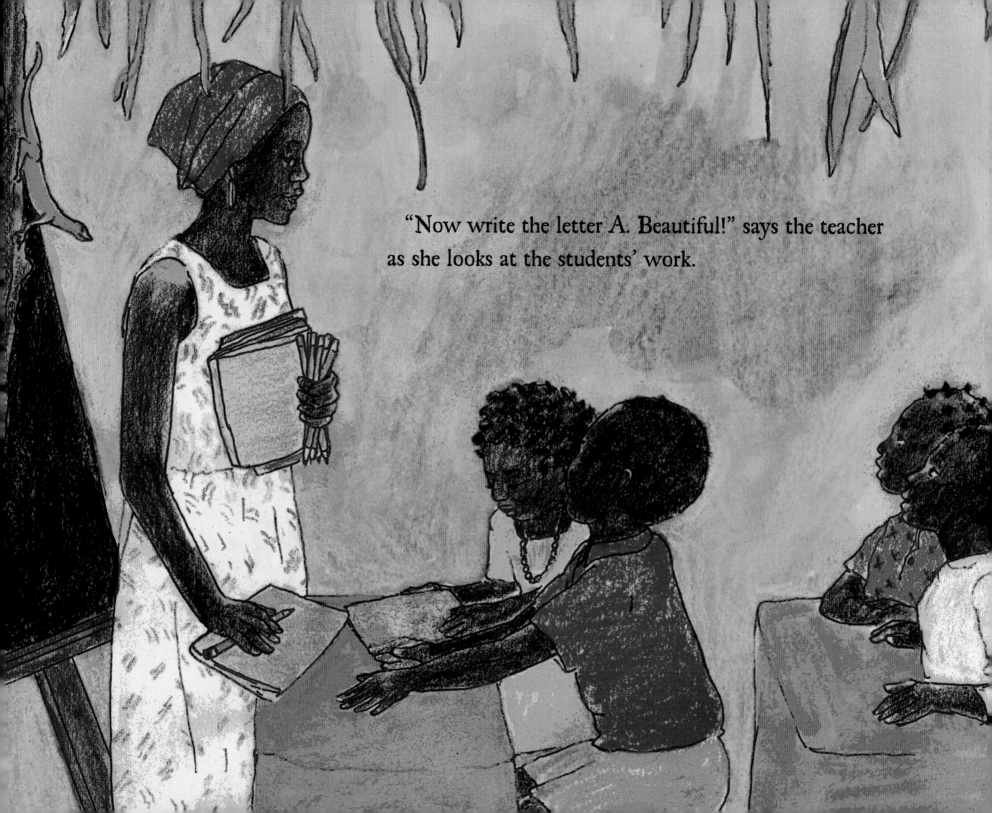

"Now write the letter A. Beautiful!" says the teacher as she looks at the students' work.

Every day Thomas learns something new.
Every day the teacher cheers him and the
other children on. "Excellent job," she says.
"Perfect, my learning friends!"

The nine months of the school year fly by.

The last day has come. The students' minds are fat with knowledge. Their notebooks are rumpled from learning.

Thomas and the other children call out, "Thank you, Teacher."

She smiles and says, "Well done, my hard-working friends! See you next year."

Thomas and the other children race home.

The school is empty, and just in time. The big rains have started.
The drops come down hard and fast.

Strong winds tear at the grass roof. The rain finds its way inside.
The school's mud walls are soaked and start to slump. The mud desks, too.

Slowly, the school disappears until there is almost nothing left.
It doesn't matter. The letters have been learned and the knowledge
taken away by the children.

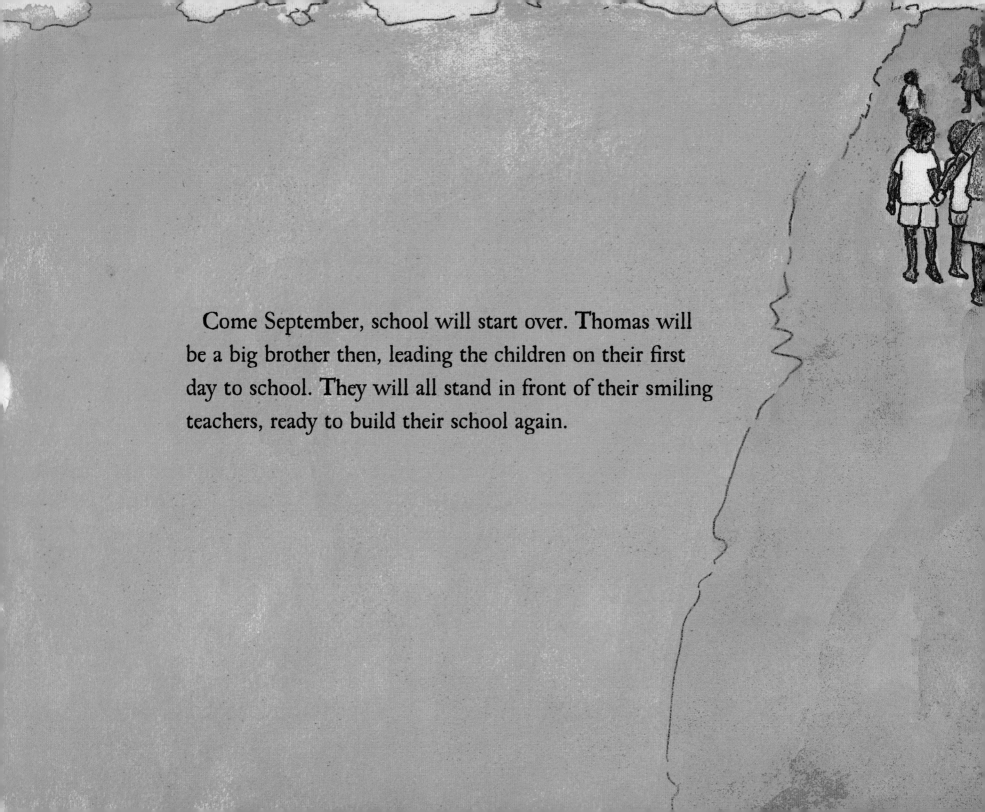

Come September, school will start over. Thomas will be a big brother then, leading the children on their first day to school. They will all stand in front of their smiling teachers, ready to build their school again.

Houghton Mifflin Books for Children is an imprint of
Houghton Mifflin Harcourt Publishing Company.
www.hmhbooks.com

The text of this book is set in 20-point Regula Antiqua.
The illustrations in this book are based on the author's
A Chuva de Manga (BrinqueBooks, São Paulo, Brazil, 2005),
with the rain scenes inspired by the art of Kitagawa Utamaro
(ca. 1752–1806) and Utagawa Hiroshige (1797–1858).
Book design by Carol Goldenberg

Library of Congress Cataloging-in-Publication Data is on file.
ISBN 978-0-547-24307-8

Manufactured in China
LEO 10 9 8 7 6 5 4 3 2 1
4500226783

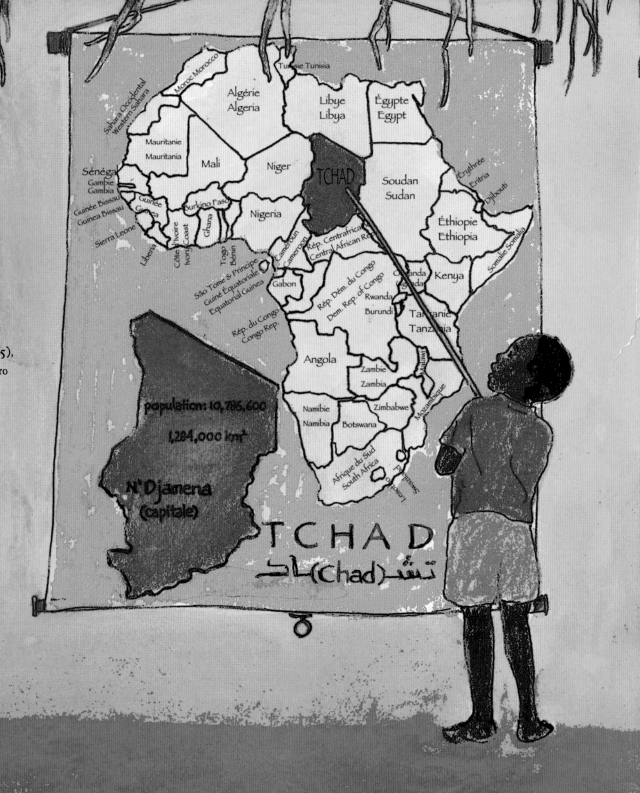